# This case

"Remember how we practiced it, girls," Mrs. Fayne said. "Hold the sides of the table and wheel the cake straight to Sara and Brett. And wait until the wedding singer introduces you."

The singer held up his mic and announced, "And now—to present the wedding cake, two of the cutest snow fairies you ever will meet!"

"That's us!" Bess said.

Nancy smiled as her friends rolled the towering wedding cake out the door.

"Cool!" whispered Nancy as she watched the cake. But her jaw dropped as she noticed something wrong. A huge chunk was missing from the back of the cake!

# Join the CLUE CREW
## & solve these other cases!

#1 *Sleepover Sleuths*

#2 *Scream for Ice Cream*

#3 *Pony Problems*

#4 *The Cinderella Ballet Mystery*

#5 *Case of the Sneaky Snowman*

#6 *The Fashion Disaster*

#7 *The Circus Scare*

#8 *Lights, Camera . . . Cats!*

#9 *The Halloween Hoax*

#10 *Ticket Trouble*

#11 *Ski School Sneak*

#12 *Valentine's Day Secret*

#13 *Chick-napped!*

#14 *The Zoo Crew*

#15 *Mall Madness*

#16 *Thanksgiving Thief*

#17 *Wedding Day Disaster*

# NANCY DREW
## #17 AND THE CLUE CREW®

## Wedding Day Disaster

### BY CAROLYN KEENE

### ILLUSTRATED BY MACKY PAMINTUAN

Aladdin Paperbacks
New York London Toronto Sydney

If you purchased this book without a cover, you should be aware that this book is stolen property. It was reported as "unsold and destroyed" to the publisher, and neither the author nor the publisher has received any payment for this "stripped book."

This book is a work of fiction. Any references to historical events, real people, or real locales are used fictitiously. Other names, characters, places, and incidents are the product of the author's imagination, and any resemblance to actual events or locales or persons, living or dead, is entirely coincidental.

🐦 ALADDIN PAPERBACKS
An imprint of Simon & Schuster Children's Publishing Division
1230 Avenue of the Americas, New York, NY 10020
Text copyright © 2008 by Simon & Schuster, Inc.
Illustrations copyright © 2008 by Macky Pamintuan
All rights reserved, including the right of reproduction in whole or in part in any form.
NANCY DREW, NANCY DREW AND THE CLUE CREW, ALADDIN PAPERBACKS, and related logo are registered trademarks of Simon & Schuster, Inc.
Designed by Lisa Vega
The text of this book was set in ITC Stone Informal.
Manufactured in the United States of America
First Aladdin Paperbacks edition November 2008
10 9 8 7 6 5 4
Library of Congress Control Number 2007943607
ISBN-13: 978-1-4169-6778-1
ISBN-10: 1-4169-6778-8

# CONTENTS

CHAPTER ONE: FLOWER POWER · · · · · · · · · · · · · · 1

CHAPTER TWO: BRAT ATTACK · · · · · · · · · · · · 13

CHAPTER THREE: SWEET REVENGE · · · · · · · · · · 22

CHAPTER FOUR: POPPED QUIZ · · · · · · · · · · · 32

CHAPTER FIVE: BUTTER SPUTTER · · · · · · · · · · 41

CHAPTER SIX: CAUGHT IN THE ACT · · · · · · · · · 45

CHAPTER SEVEN: HIDE AND PEEK · · · · · · · · · · · 53

CHAPTER EIGHT: NOSE KNOWS · · · · · · · · · · · 61

CHAPTER NINE: ART SMART · · · · · · · · · · · · 67

CHAPTER TEN: CASE CRACKED · · · · · · · · · · 79

# CHAPTER ONE

## Flower Power

"Should I drop one petal at a time," eight-year-old Nancy Drew asked, "or two at a time?"

Nancy's best friends, Bess Marvin and George Fayne, stood by her as she lifted her white basket of rose petals.

"Here's what you do," George said. She put her arm around Nancy's shoulder. "Grab yourself a fistful, swing your arm all the way back . . . and throw!"

George's cousin Bess Marvin rolled her blue eyes. "Nancy is a flower girl at a wedding, George," she said. "Not a pitcher in a Little League game!"

Nancy smiled. Being a flower girl at a wedding

1

was just one of her dreams. And that Friday night it was about to come true!

Her cousin Sara was marrying a fun guy named Brett. Because it was winter, Sara had planned a snowball wedding, where the whole wedding party would wear white. Nancy was wearing a pretty white flower girl dress.

A waitress dashed by the girls, balancing a platter on one hand. More waiters and waitresses were setting up plates of hors d'oeuvres on long, fancily decorated tables. In about fifteen minutes the guests would arrive at the Chapel of Love for the wedding. In about an hour the wedding ceremony would begin!

"It's cool your mom is catering Sara's wedding, George," Nancy said. "This way you and Bess can be at the wedding too!"

George's mom ran Fayne's Catering Service in River Heights. Besides ordering and preparing the food, Mrs. Fayne liked to add special touches. Tonight she had Bess and George dress up like snow fairies. Together they would wheel out the wedding cake during the reception.

Bess twirled in her white dress decorated with silver snowflakes. "I feel so pretty in this dress!" she exclaimed. "I want to be a snow fairy forever!"

"Forever?" George groaned. She straightened the white tiara over her dark curls. "Can you picture solving mysteries in these frilly clothes?"

Nancy giggled at the thought. She, Bess, and George had their own detective club called the Clue Crew. They loved solving mysteries more than anything!

"Hi, girls," Mrs. Fayne said as she walked over carrying a platter. She turned to two waiters standing around talking. "The spinach pies are ready to be set up, please."

"Did someone say spinach pies?" a voice boomed.

Nancy turned around. Walking over was Bob Kernkraut, the owner of the Chapel of Love. He was wearing a white suit and a dark blue tie decorated with white snowmen.

"Would you like a spinach pie, Bob?" asked Mrs. Fayne.

Mr. Kernkraut stared at the platter. Then he quickly shook his head and said, "Oh, no thank you. My wife put me on the Waist Watchers Diet—so no more snacks for me!"

Mr. Kernkraut walked away as a waiter grabbed the platter. Mrs. Fayne then smiled at the girls and asked, "Who wants to see the wedding cake?"

Three hands shot up.

"Follow me!" Mrs. Fayne said.

On the way to the kitchen, George nodded toward Mr. Kernkraut. He was leaning against one of the tables with a deviled egg in one hand. His eyes darted around the room as he quickly stuffed it in his mouth.

"Some diet," George murmured.

Mrs. Fayne stopped in front of the kitchen door before opening it. "Don't go too near the cake, girls," she warned. "Famous François is putting on the finishing touches."

"Who is Famous François?" Bess asked.

"Are you kidding, Bess?" George said. "He's the most famous baker in River Heights—maybe the world!"

"And don't say the word 'baker'!" added Mrs. Fayne. "Famous François is a cake 'artist' with his own studio."

"Is it a cake or the *Mona Lisa*?" Bess sighed.

Mrs. Fayne opened the door wide. The girls stepped inside the kitchen and gasped. On a round table in front of them was the most beautiful wedding cake they had ever seen. Its seven layers were frosted snowy white. Sticking out from the cream were tiny silver twigs that looked like winter trees.

"Awesome!" Nancy exclaimed.

A man wearing a chef's hat stood on a ladder

5

as he hung what looked like icicles from the cake. Standing beside him was a teenage girl, holding more icicles in a pan.

"It is my Matrimonial Mountain of Love!" François announced with a French accent. "It represents the heights to which a couple must climb to reach true happiness!"

"To me it represents something yummy!" George said, licking her lips.

Famous François sniffed as he grabbed the last icicle. The girl put down the empty pan and said to the three friends, "Speaking of yummy, how about a cookie?"

She lifted a plate filled with white snowflake-shaped cookies. She was dressed in all white too—from her smock to her canvas sneakers.

"My daughter Adele will be a famous pastry artist someday too," François said. "Just like her famous papa!"

"Dad!" said Adele, blushing.

Mrs. Fayne gave the girls permission to take one cookie each. As they nibbled, the door flew open. Sara, in her beautiful bridal gown, stepped into the kitchen. Behind her was a girl who looked about seven years old.

"Why can't I be the flower girl, Sara?" the girl asked in a whiny voice. "I'm Brett's next-door neighbor!"

"We told you, Kendall," Sara said. "My cousin Nancy is the flower girl."

"Hi, Kendall!" Nancy said with a smile and a wave.

Kendall didn't smile back. She marched over to the cake and dragged her finger across the frosting. The cake shook as the table shifted on its wheels.

"No touching the master-piece!" François cried.

Kendall's nose wrinkled as she licked her finger. "Buttercream!" She gagged. "I hate butter! Now I won't be able to eat the cake!"

But Sara was not paying attention to Kendall. Her eyes were fixed on the top of the wedding cake.

"Isn't there supposed to be a bride and groom on top of my cake?" Sara asked. "Instead there are two dogs!"

Nancy looked up too. Sure enough, two gray dogs topped François's Mountain of Love.

"They are not dogs!" François snapped with a wave of his hand. "They are the ice wolves of Patagonia."

"Okay," said Sara slowly. "But I asked you for a bride and groom."

"Yeah, Dad," Adele said. "It's Sara's wedding cake. And a bride's wedding should always be perfect."

Famous François stuck his chin in the air. "No ice wolves—no Famous François!" he declared.

Sara seemed to blink back tears. "It's fine," she said. "Keep the ice wolves where they are."

She then picked up her hem, turned around, and left the kitchen.

*It's not fine*, Nancy thought sadly. *Sara hates it.*

"Hey, you guys," said Adele, trying to smile. "Look what else my dad and I baked."

The teenager pointed to more pastries on the butcher-block table. On it sat a cheesecake, a fluffy lemon meringue pie, and some white frosted cupcakes.

"The cupcakes will circle the bottom of the cake," Adele explained. "To look like fallen snow."

"Everything looks delicious," Nancy said. "Right, Kendall?"

But when Nancy turned around, Kendall was gone.

"That's funny," said Mrs. Fayne, looking around the kitchen. "What happened to that onion I was about to cut?"

The girls left the kitchen. Guests were starting to arrive for the wedding. Nancy's father had come with his brand-new camcorder. Mr. Drew was a lawyer, but tonight he was pretending to be a big-shot movie director!

"Sara and Brett's wedding—take one!" Mr. Drew boomed. He pointed the camera straight at Nancy. "The prettiest little flower girl in the whole wide world!"

"Thank you!" Nancy said with a little curtsy.

Mr. Drew turned his camera toward some other relatives. Just then a bridesmaid named Natalie ran over. "Nancy, the ceremony is starting in a few minutes," she said. "Sara wants the wedding party to line up."

Nancy's tummy fluttered with butterflies. "This is it!" she told her friends. "Where did I put my basket of rose petals?"

Bess pointed to Nancy's basket, sitting on a nearby chair. "There!" she said.

Nancy grabbed her basket, then raced to join the others. The bridesmaids and ushers were excitedly whispering to one another. Nancy thought she was the luckiest of them all. She got to stand in front of Sara and her father, Nancy's Uncle Bob.

"Good luck, Nancy," Sara whispered.

"You too!" Nancy whispered back. But as the organ music began to play in the chapel, her nose began to itch.

As Nancy sniffed, Uncle Bob whispered, "It's okay to cry at weddings, Nancy."

Nancy nodded, but she knew she wasn't crying. So why were her eyes watering?

The bridesmaids and ushers walked side-by-side down the long white carpet. Finally it was Nancy's turn. She gave a big sniff, flashed a smile, and began her walk.

"Oh, look, it's the flower girl!" someone pointed out.

"She has reddish blond hair, just like Sara!" another voice murmured.

Nancy's watery eyes burned as she sprinkled petals on the carpet, just like she had in the rehearsal. But as she dropped the petals, she no longer smelled roses. Instead she smelled some-thing not flowery at all!

Nancy glanced down at her basket and gulped. Under all the beautiful white rose petals . . . was a big peeled raw *onion*!

# Chapter Two

## Brat Attack

*Omigosh*! Nancy thought. She gritted her teeth as she tried to keep smiling. *How did this get in here?*

Nancy made her way up the aisle. Through her watery eyes she could see Kendall sitting at the edge of the aisle. She was smiling meanly straight at her!

*The revenge of the wannabe flower girl!* Nancy thought grimly. She finally reached the end the long white carpet, where she stood next to the bridesmaids.

"What's that smell?" one bridesmaid whispered.

"Were you eating onion dip?" another murmured.

"Here Comes the Bride" began to play. Sara looked stunning as she walked down the aisle with her father. But Nancy felt awful. What should have been a dream come true had become a true nightmare!

Nancy tried not to sniff or wipe her tears during the ceremony. She tried not to look at Kendall, either.

"I now pronounce you husband and wife!" said the minister.

Brett tenderly kissed Sara. The organ played and the wedding party began filing back down the white carpet.

"Gotcha!" Kendall snickered as Nancy walked by.

Once outside the chapel, Nancy hugged her dad. "Do you think you're allergic to roses, honey?" he asked.

"No, Daddy," Nancy said. She didn't want to

tell her father about Kendall. She didn't want anyone to make a fuss and spoil Sara's wedding.

Instead Nancy ran to throw away the onion. Then she went straight to Bess and George to tell them what happened.

"She ruined it!" Nancy wailed. "Kendall stuck an onion in my basket and ruined my big flower-girl moment!"

Bess pointed to Kendall, plucking flowers out of a fancy flower arrangement. "I wouldn't be surprised if she ruins the whole wedding!" she said.

"Should we tell someone?" asked George.

"No," Nancy said, still not wanting to spoil the wedding. "All I want to do is wash my stinky hands!"

The girls rushed to the ladies' room. Nancy washed her hands three times. But when she turned off the faucet, she heard someone crying. Bess and George whispered that they heard it too.

"It can't be the onion," Nancy said softly. "I threw it away before I came in!"

The door to one of the stalls opened. A woman stepped out, dabbing her eyes. Nancy recognized her at once.

"Aren't you Patsy?" Nancy asked. "From Patsy's Pastries on River Street?"

"Wow!" said Bess. "You once baked pink and white cupcakes for my birthday party!"

"Your cupcakes rock!" George added.

"Thank you," Patsy said. "I'm also Brett's aunt."

"He's lucky he has an aunt who can bake!" said Nancy.

"Tell him that," Patsy sniffled. "I wanted to bake the wedding cake. But instead he asked the Famous François!"

Nancy, Bess, and George exchanged surprised glances.

"Um," George said slowly, "maybe it's because François bakes wedding cakes and you bake cupcakes—"

"What's a wedding cake, anyway?" Patsy cut in. "A supersize cupcake with a bride and groom stuck on top?"

"Ice wolves," Bess told her. "Famous François put ice wolves on top of the cake."

"Wolves?" Aunt Patsy sobbed.

Nancy didn't know what else to do. So she

and her friends quietly left the ladies' room.

"I don't get it." Bess sighed. "If I had an aunt like Patsy, I'd have a cupcake wedding dress!"

Nancy looked around the reception hall. It was decorated with white balloons and flowers. The band was playing their first song, and guests had begun to dance. As the girls watched a couple twirling across the dance floor, Nancy saw Famous François and Adele wheeling the wedding cake out of the kitchen on a rolling cart. Adele held open the door to another room as François pushed it inside.

"Where are they putting the cake?" Nancy asked.

"François wants to keep the cake in a special room instead of the kitchen," said George. "That's what my mom told me before the wedding."

"At least it will be safe from Kendall!" Bess snorted.

Nancy forgot all about Kendall and the onion

as she enjoyed the reception. She watched Sara and Brett dance their first dance as husband and wife. Then Nancy stood on her dad's shoes as they danced together too.

The guests sat down for a delicious wedding dinner. While the plates were being cleared away, the band struck up a fast song. Bess and George ran over to Nancy so they could dance their favorite line dance, the Electric Train.

"And now," Mr. Drew said, pointing his camera at the girls, "it's time for—Dancing with the Wedding Stars!"

"Oh, Daddy!" Nancy giggled.

Mrs. Fayne hurried over. "I need my little snow fairies!" she said. "It's time to bring out the cake!"

"Yay!" Nancy exclaimed. She was just as excited as Bess and George as she ran to the cake room with them. The door was already open as they all rushed inside. Mrs. Fayne wheeled the cake away from the wall.

"Remember how we practiced it, girls," Mrs. Fayne said. "Bess, you stand on one side of the table. George, you stand on the other. Hold the sides of the table and wheel the cake straight to Sara and Brett."

"Check!" said George as they took their places.

"And wait until the wedding singer introduces you," Mrs. Fayne reminded the girls.

Nancy wanted to do something to help. She held the door as Mrs. Fayne stepped out first. Nancy could see her whispering to the wedding singer. The singer held up his mike and announced, "And now—to present the wedding cake, two of the cutest snow fairies you ever will meet!"

"That's us!" Bess said.

Nancy smiled as her friends rolled the towering wedding cake out the door. The wedding singer began belting out a song called "Mountain of Love."

"Cool!" whispered Nancy as she watched the cake. But her jaw dropped as she noticed something wrong. A huge chunk was missing from the back of the cake!

# CHAPTER THREE

## Sweet Revenge

*Oh, noooo!* Nancy told herself. *I've got to tell Mrs. Fayne!*

Nancy raced like the wind after the cake. But on the way, her Aunt Iris grabbed her to give her a sloppy kiss.

"Excuse me, Aunt Iris," Nancy said politely.

She broke away and kept running. But the cake was already standing in front of Sara and Brett!

"The bride cuts the cake!" the wedding singer sang. "The bride cuts the cake. . . ."

Sara beamed as she picked up the knife. She was about to cut when her arm froze.

"The cake!" she exclaimed. "Brett, someone took a piece of our cake!"

"No way!" said Brett.

Bess and George ran around the table to see what Sara was talking about.

"Whoa!" George declared when she saw the missing chunk. "Someone must have been hungry!"

"I like to fix things," said Bess, staring at the cake. "But even I can't fix that!"

The guests began crowding around the cake and the couple. Mrs. Fayne shouldered her way through the crowd. When she saw the cake, she turned as white as the frosting!

"I don't understand!" Mrs. Fayne gasped.

"The cake was in the cake room all through dinner!"

Nancy ran over to Bess and George. She could see the crowd part as Famous François pushed his way to the cake.

The cake artist gasped and clutched his chest when he saw the missing piece.

"I don't know how this happened, François," Mrs. Fayne said. "I really don't!"

"I do!" François shot back. "This is what happens when you allow children to play around food!"

"We didn't do it!" George insisted.

"We just wheeled the cake out," explained Bess. "That was our job as snow fairies."

"And I held the door!" Nancy added.

"Hey, it's okay," Brett said. He tried to force a little chuckle. "Maybe someone couldn't resist a little bite because it looked so good!"

"Little bite?" cried Sara. "It's like a bulldozer plowed through it!"

"Sara—," Brett started to say.

"I'm sorry, Brett," Sara cut in, sniffing back a tear. "But this is my wedding, and I wanted everything to be perfect."

A chorus of "awww"s filled the room. But Kendall didn't seem sad for Sara at all. She was giggling meanly!

"Well, I wanted my cake to be perfect too!" Famous François exclaimed. "Therefore I don't want anyone eating it the way it is!"

Nancy saw Adele standing with the guests. Her eyes darted around the room nervously, as if she was embarrassed by her dad.

"Wait a minute, François" Mr. Kernkraut called out. "If the guests can't eat wedding cake, what will they eat?"

Famous François threw back his head and declared, "Let them eat cheesecake!"

Adele followed her father as he huffed out of the room. The guests whispered and mumbled among themselves.

"Peter, Erica," Mrs. Fayne wearily told two waiters, "wheel the cake back into the cake room, please."

As the cake was whisked away, the wedding singer smiled and began to sing, "Because you had a bad day . . ."

Nancy saw her father speaking quietly to Mrs. Fayne.

"If you ever need a lawyer, I'm here," Mr. Drew said.

"Thanks." Mrs. Fayne sighed.

George turned to Nancy and Bess. "This stinks," she said with a frown. "Famous François blamed my mom in front of everybody!"

"He blamed us, too," Bess pointed out.

"I know," said Nancy. "And it wasn't our fault. Or Mrs. Fayne's!"

"Then what happened to the cake?" George asked.

Nancy thought about the huge chunk missing from the cake. It couldn't have just fallen off!

"I think someone ruined it on purpose,"

Nancy whispered. "And it's up to the Clue Crew to find out."

George narrowed her eyes at Kendall. The flower-girl wannabe was still having a good laugh over the ruined cake.

"Kendall has been making trouble ever since the wedding started!" said George.

"Yeah," Bess agreed. "Remember the stinky onion in your basket?"

Nancy nodded. How could she forget? "Come on," she said. "Let's see what Kendall has to say."

Kendall flashed a mean grin as the girls walked over. "Did you see what happened?" Kendall asked. "Whoever heard of a wedding without a wedding cake?"

"Thanks to you!" snapped George.

"You already stuck an onion in my flower basket," Nancy said angrily. "Did you cut a chunk of the cake and eat it too?"

Kendall groaned as she shook her head. "I told you!" she said. "I hate buttercream. I hate anything with butter in it. So there!"

She whirled around and left in a huff.

"How do we know she really hates butter?" George asked.

"Kendall didn't have to eat it," Bess pointed out. "She could have cut a piece and thrown it away!"

"We didn't see a slice of cake anywhere," said Nancy. "But I'm sure we'll find other clues."

So while the others sat down to eat cheesecake, the girls headed to the scene of the crime to look for clues.

Nancy opened the door to the cake room, where the wedding cake stood alone. This time the missing slice faced the outside instead of the wall.

"What do we know so far?" Nancy asked.

Bess stuck her finger inside the gap and gave it a lick. "That the cake has cherry filling!" she said.

"Bess!" George complained. "Don't eat the evidence!"

Nancy walked over to the cart. On the silver-colored tablecloth was a creamy smear. The cream was white with streaks of dark pink through it.

"It's shaped like a footprint," Nancy said. She pointed to the side of the cake. "And it's right in front of the missing chunk!"

"White like the frosting, pink like the cherry filling," Bess observed. Her eyebrows flew up. "Do you think someone kicked a hole in the cake?"

"I don't think so," said Nancy. "It looks like someone cut out a neat slice."

"I don't get it," George said, staring at the creamy footprint. "If someone did cut the cake, why would they step up on the table to do it?"

"Kendall is bratty enough to climb furniture," Bess suggested.

"No," Nancy said, shaking her head. "That footprint is way too big to be Kendall's.

"I still think Kendall did it," said George, frowning. "She was mad at Sara and Brett for not making her the flower girl."

"Who else would be mad at Sara and Brett?" asked Bess. "They're both so nice!"

Nancy thought the same thing. Until she remembered what she heard in the washroom.

"Brett's Aunt Patsy!" Nancy blurted out. "She was upset that she wasn't picked to bake the wedding cake."

"Wow!" George said. "Would she ruin the wedding cake to get even?"

"No way," said Bess. "Aunt Patsy is as sweet as her cupcakes!"

After thinking about Aunt Patsy, Nancy agreed with Bess. She was too nice to do anything so horrible—especially to her own nephew.

Just then Mr. Drew stuck his head in the door.

"Come on, girls!" he said. "Sara is about to throw the bouquet!"

Nancy let out a little gasp. They couldn't miss that!

On the way out, Nancy checked out a small trash can for any used paper plates or napkins. Instead she found a dark blue tie decorated with white snowmen.

Nancy studied the tie as she pulled it out. Smack in the middle was a huge smudge—a creamy white smudge!

"What is it, Nancy?" Bess asked.

Nancy smiled as she said, "Another clue!"

# CHAPTER FOUR

## Popped Quiz

"Hey," said George, looking closer at the tie. "Doesn't that tie belong to Mr. Kernkraut?"

"Yes!" Nancy said as she remembered. "His tie was dark blue with snowmen on it."

"Mr. Kernkraut must have been here inside the cake room," Bess pointed out. "Maybe his tie got messy when he ate a piece of the cake."

"Why didn't Mr. Kernkraut just wait until Sara and Brett cut the cake?" George wondered. "It's his wedding hall. I'm sure they would have given him a piece."

"Because he told everyone he's on a diet," said Nancy. "And we already caught him snacking on the job!"

The girls wanted to keep the tie as a clue. So they ran into the kitchen, where Mrs. Fayne gave them a plastic zip-top bag. Nancy quickly put the cream-covered tie into the bag. George placed it in her mom's tote bag for safekeeping.

"This is a mystery, all right." Mrs. Fayne shook her head.

Nancy nodded. But then she thought of a question for George's mother.

"Do you think anyone working for you cut the cake by mistake?" Nancy asked in a low voice.

Mrs. Fayne shook her head.

"I spoke to all my waiters about the cake," she said. "They were too busy serving dinner when it happened."

"My mom's waiters are very honest," George added.

But as they left the kitchen, George said, "There's just one thing I don't get. If someone did cut a big chunk out of the cake—where is the knife?"

The girls joined the other guests just as Sara

was tossing the bouquet. Kendall ran behind Sara, jumped up, and practically grabbed the bouquet out of her hand.

"I caught it!" Kendall squealed, waving it in the air. "Look! I caught it!"

"Give me a break," muttered George.

Sara was smiling, but Nancy had a feeling she was still sad about her wedding cake.

*Don't worry, Sara,* Nancy thought. *The Clue Crew is on the case!*

As the winter sun came up Saturday morning, Nancy slept late. She was tired from the wedding the night before. But the minute her eyes popped open, she was ready for a new day—and a new case!

"How do you spell 'Kernkraut'?" George asked later as she typed on Nancy's computer.

The Clue Crew's detective headquarters were up in Nancy's bedroom. George was a computer whiz and insisted on entering all the suspects and clues.

"I think it's spelled kind of like sauerkraut," Nancy said.

George nodded as she typed their suspects: Mr. Kernkraut, the hungry wedding hall owner, and Kendall, the jilted flower girl. Aunt Patsy was still too nice to be a suspect.

Bess was sitting on the rug and trying on Nancy's flower-girl shoes.

"Maybe Kendall lied about hating butter so we wouldn't think she ate the cake," she suggested. "I wish we could find out if she really hates butter."

Nancy sat on the edge of her bed. She tossed her pillow in the air as she thought.

"We should ask Kendall more questions," Nancy said. "But first we have to find out where she lives."

"How are we going to do that?" asked Bess. "I don't even think she goes to our school."

"Kendall said she was Brett's next-door neighbor," Nancy remembered. "So all we have to do is find out where Brett lives!"

"Okay," George said. She turned around in

her chair and smiled. "But I think I have a better way to spend the morning."

George pulled three papers from her jeans pocket. "Ta-da! My mom bought us gift certificates to the movies for helping at the wedding yesterday!"

"Cool!" said Bess. *"Henry the Hero Hound* is playing at the River Heights Cineplex. We can make the first show!"

"What do you think, Nancy?" George asked.

Nancy wanted to work on their new case that morning. But she also wanted to see *Henry the Hero Hound.*

"I think even detectives need a movie break once in a while," Nancy said with a smile. "Let's go!"

When it came to going out, the girls all had the same rules. They could walk or ride their bikes five blocks away from their houses as long as they were together. The Cineplex was ten blocks away, so Hannah Gruen offered to drive them there.

Hannah had been the Drews' housekeeper since Nancy's mother died when she was only three years old. Hannah couldn't take the place of Nancy's mother, but she came pretty close!

"You all have your popcorn," Hannah said inside the movie theater. "Stay right in your seats while I get myself something to snack on."

"Okay, Hannah," Nancy agreed.

As Hannah made her way up the aisle, Nancy looked around the theater. It was packed with kids, all there to see *Henry the Hero Hound.*

"Mmmm!" George said as she dug into her bag of popcorn. "Extra-buttered popcorn! That Kendall doesn't know what she's missing!"

"Speaking of Kendall," Bess hissed, "guess who's sitting right behind us?"

Nancy didn't have to guess. She could hear Kendall's whiny voice filling the theater.

"I told you, Vicky! I wanted the jumbo-size popcorn, not the regular size!"

Nancy glanced back. She saw Kendall sitting next to a teenage girl.

"Your parents told me to buy you the regular size," said Vicky. "So can you just deal with it?"

"Some babysitter you are, Icky Vicky!" Kendall snapped as she dug noisily into her popcorn. The bag was resting on the arm of her chair.

Suddenly Nancy got an idea.

"I want to give Kendall a little pop quiz," Nancy whispered to Bess and George. "Pop as in popcorn!"

"What do you mean?" Bess whispered back.

"Go over to Kendall and keep her busy, you guys," Nancy explained. "Don't let her eat or look at her popcorn."

Bess and George traded shrugs. They stood up, then made their way down the next row to Kendall.

"Hey!" Kendall said when she saw Bess and George. "You're those goofy fairies from the wedding yesterday!"

"Yeah, and guess what?" said George. "There's someone here who thinks you're being a brat!"

"Who?" Kendall demanded. She stood up and looked around the theater. "Who said that about me?"

"She's wearing a red sweater and a matching headband," Bess said, pointing to the back of the theater.

"Help me find her, Vicky!" Kendall demanded.

"Whatever." Vicky groaned as she stood up too. While she and Kendall looked to the back of the theater, Nancy grabbed George's extra-buttered popcorn. Then she reached way back and switched Kendall's bag with George's.

Hurrying back to her seat, Nancy sat down and called, "Bess, George! The movie is going to start any minute!"

Bess and George turned to leave Kendall.

"Wait!" Kendall said. "You have to help me find that girl with the red headband!"

"What girl?" asked George.

"Enjoy the show," Bess said with a smile.

Kendall looked confused as Bess and George returned to their row.

"Did you just do what I think you did?" George whispered as they sat down.

Nancy answered with a sly smile. The lights

in the theater began to dim just as Hannah returned with a box of peanuts.

"The line at the concession stand was a mile long!" Hannah said, sitting down. "I thought I'd miss the movie!"

The curtain rose slowly in front of the screen. But Nancy wasn't watching the previews. She was glancing back at Kendall as she stuffed a handful of popcorn into her mouth.

"Five . . . four . . . three," Nancy whispered, counting down. "Two . . . one!"

"Bllllech!!!" Kendall cried. She jumped up and clapped her hand over her mouth. "B-b-butter! B-b-butter! Blllech!!"

# CHAPTER FIVE

## Butter Sputter

"What's the matter with that poor girl?" Hannah whispered as Kendall spit pieces of popcorn on the floor.

"I guess she hates butter after all." Nancy chuckled.

The girls took their minds off the case to watch *Henry the Hero Hound*. After the movie, Hannah drove them straight back to their detective headquarters.

"Should we take Kendall off our suspect list?" George asked as she opened their case file. "She wasn't lying about hating butter."

"She still could have ruined the cake just to be bratty," Bess pointed out.

"True," said Nancy. "But that footprint we found was way too big to be Kendall's, remember?"

"And remember how clean Kendall's dress was?" Bess asked. "With a big chunk of cake like that, she would have gotten messy for sure!"

"She's got a big mouth, too, remember?" George said. But she deleted Kendall's name from their suspect list.

"That leaves us with Mr. Kernkraut," Nancy concluded. "And we have his messy tie to prove it!"

Mr. Drew smiled as he stepped into the room. Nancy's chocolate Labrador puppy, Chocolate Chip, scampered after him.

"How was the movie?" Mr. Drew asked.

"Awesome, Daddy!" said Nancy. "Henry the Hero Hound sniffed a boy's sneaker—then tracked him all the way to the woods where he was lost!"

Chip jumped up on Nancy and wagged her tail.

"You're a good dog too, Chip!" Nancy said, just in case her puppy was jealous.

"Well," Mr. Drew announced with a smile, "I have another blockbuster film downstairs you might like."

"Which one?" asked George.

"The film I took at the wedding last night!" Mr. Drew said. "Starring Nancy, Bess, and George!"

All three girls thundered down the stairs to the Drews' den. They sat in front of the TV screen to watch the wedding movie. They giggled when they saw themselves dancing the Electric Train.

Suddenly Nancy noticed something in the background. A woman was stepping out of the cake room.

Grabbing the remote, Nancy pressed the pause button. She wiggled closer to the screen, pointed, and said, "Look, isn't that Aunt Patsy?"

"What was she doing in the cake room?" asked Bess.

Nancy practically pressed her nose against

the screen as she looked closer. There was some-thing in Aunt Patsy's hands. It looked like a purple container—the plastic kind that Hannah kept leftovers in.

"If you ask me," Nancy said slowly, "Aunt Patsy is taking the cake!"

# ChaPTER Six

## Caught in the Act

Nancy pressed play. They watched as Aunt Patsy carefully shut the door behind her, then walked away with the purple container.

"Aunt Patsy can't be a suspect," Bess said. "She's so nice!"

"Then she's a nice suspect," said George. She turned to Nancy. "Do you think Aunt Patsy still has that piece of cake?"

"Probably not," Nancy said. "But we should go to her bakery today."

"For cupcakes?" asked Bess excitedly.

"For clues!" Nancy answered with a smile.

The girls ran upstairs, where George added Aunt Patsy to their suspect list. Then they got permission to walk together to River Street. The girls were lucky that River Street was within their five-block range. The wide street had the best stores and places to eat—like Patsy's Pastries!

As Nancy, Bess, and George walked toward the bakery, they spotted Adele. Famous François's daughter was walking into Dapper Duds Dry Cleaners with something white draped over her arm.

"Let's say hi to Adele," Nancy suggested. "Maybe she found out something about the cake."

The three friends entered the cleaners. Adele was handing her white smock over the counter to the store owner, Mr. Petruzzi.

"What is this stain?" Mr. Petruzzi asked as he held up the smock. "Some kind of whipped cream?"

"It's buttercream," Adele answered. Her eyes widened when the girls stepped up to the counter.

"Hi, Adele," Nancy said. "Sorry about your dad's cake yesterday."

"Thanks," said Adele. She paid Mr. Petruzzi and turned to leave. The girls darted in front of her before she reached the door.

"Adele, did you see anything weird before the cake was ruined?" George asked.

"Like somebody hanging around the cake?" Bess added.

"Or sneaking into the cake room?" Nancy put in.

"No!" answered Adele. "Nothing weird at all."

"Excuse me, miss!" Mr. Petruzzi called. "These were in the pocket of your smock."

Mr. Petruzzi held up two miniature plastic figurines. They were a bride and a groom!

"Whoops!" Adele said. She ran back and grabbed the figurines. Then,

47

with a quick good-bye to the girls, she left the store.

The girls left the store too. Nancy watched as Adele made her way up River Street.

"What were a bride and groom doing in Adele's pocket?" Nancy asked. "I thought her dad wanted those silly ice wolves!"

"Maybe Adele is saving them for her own wedding!" said Bess cheerily.

Patsy's Pastries was a few stores away from the dry cleaners. The girls stopped in front of the door before going in.

"If Aunt Patsy still has the cake," Nancy said, "it's probably in her refrigerator."

"The fridge is in the back room," said George. "I helped my mom pick up pastries for a party once."

A bell above the door jingled as the girls stepped inside. The store was warm and smelled sugary sweet.

Aunt Patsy came out from the back room. In her hand was a CLOSED sign.

"Oh, hello, girls," Aunt Patsy said. "I was just about to close the store."

"But it's the middle of the day," said Nancy.

"I know," Aunt Patsy said as she hung the sign on the door. "But I have some important business to take care of."

The girls exchanged worried glances. How would they go into the back room if Aunt Patsy was closing the store?

"Come back tomorrow," Aunt Patsy told the girls, holding the door wide open. "I'll have cupcakes fresh out of the oven!"

Nancy couldn't take her eye off the back room as they made their way to the door. They were about to step outside when Aunt Patsy's phone rang.

"I'd better get that," Aunt Patsy said. She left the girls to answer the phone on the countertop. "Patsy's Pastries, how can I help you?"

The second Aunt Patsy turned her back, Nancy whispered, "Let's go."

Very quietly the girls slipped past Aunt Patsy

into the back room. A huge stainless steel refrigerator stood against the wall. In the middle of the room was a wooden table. On the table was a plate of frosted cupcakes.

"Are we lucky or what?" Bess said, running toward the cupcakes. "I want strawberry!"

"Stop, Bess!" Nancy hissed. "We're not here to eat cupcakes. We're here to find the missing piece of wedding cake!"

Bess looked disappointed as they passed the table to get to the refrigerator. Nancy grabbed the handle and pulled the door wide open. Peering inside, she saw a stack of cardboard boxes, bowls of frosting, and—

"The purple container!" Nancy whispered.

She reached inside for the container. It looked exactly like the container Aunt Patsy was holding in the wedding movie.

"The missing chunk of cake is probably in there," George said. "Open it, Nancy!"

Nancy was starting to pry the lid off when she heard voices. Bess and George heard them too.

"Hide," George whispered.

Quickly Nancy, Bess, and George slipped behind the side of the refrigerator. As the voices got louder, they scrunched closer together.

"Where are we going?" asked a kid's voice.

"You'll find out," Aunt Patsy's voice said. "But remember, what happens back here stays back here!"

Nancy raised an eyebrow at Bess and George. What was going on?

The girls peeked out from behind the refrigerator. Nancy gasped. Three kids from their third-grade class at River Heights Elementary School were sitting around the table. They were Quincy Taylor, Marcy Rubin, and Kayla Bruce. And they were all wearing blindfolds!

# ChAPTER SEVEN

## Hide and Peek

"I smell cupcakes!" said Quincy.

Aunt Patsy let out a chuckle. But Nancy wasn't laughing as she turned to her friends.

"What are they doing?" Nancy asked.

"I wore a blindfold when I played Pin the Tail on the Donkey," whispered Bess. "Maybe they're going to play too!"

"Or maybe," George whispered slowly, "they're Aunt Patsy's prisoners!"

The girls ducked behind the refrigerator. Aunt Patsy was walking toward it!

"Keep your blindfolds on, kids," Aunt Patsy called. "I need to get one more thing."

Nancy felt a rush of cold air as Aunt Patsy

opened the refrigerator door. She couldn't see Aunt Patsy. But she could hear her cry out, "Cheese and crackers! What happened to the container?"

Startled, Nancy dropped the purple container. It made a clunking noise as it rolled across the floor.

"Rats!" said Nancy between gritted teeth.

"I think somebody is back there!" Aunt Patsy called in a singsong voice. "Come out, come out, whoever you are!"

Nancy sucked in her breath. Why did she have to be such a klutz? She stepped out first, followed by Bess and George.

"I thought you girls had left," Aunt Patsy said.

"We were just leaving!" Bess blurted. "But if we could grab some cupcakes on our way out . . ."

"No!" George interrupted. She threw back her shoulders as she looked Aunt Patsy in the eye. "We have important business too. We have to find the missing piece of Famous François's wedding cake."

Nancy pointed to the container on the floor. "And we think we found it," she said.

George turned to the kids at the table and shouted, "Run while you can! We'll take care of her!"

But the kids, still blindfolded, didn't move.

"That sounds like Nancy, Bess, and George!" said Marcy.

"Must be another mystery," Kayla said.

Aunt Patsy tilted her head. "Hmmm," she said. "So you girls thought I took the piece from that wedding cake!"

"My dad caught you on his camcorder coming out of the cake room," Nancy explained gently. "You were carrying that purple container."

"I did go into the cake room, but not for cake," Aunt Patsy said. "That nice girl Adele invited me to take one of her father's cupcakes."

"Cupcakes?" Nancy asked.

"Yes," replied Aunt Patsy. "Mr. Kernkraut unlocked the door and let me in."

Aunt Patsy picked up the container. She pried

off the lid, reached inside, and pulled out a cupcake with white frosting. It was the same type
of cupcake that had circled the bottom of the
cake.

"It's a bit lopsided from the fall," Aunt Patsy
said. "But it shouldn't affect the way it tastes."

"All this talk about cupcakes is making my
mouth water!" Quincy complained.

"Bring it on!" Marcy declared.

Nancy looked at the kids, then at Aunt Patsy. "What's going on?" she asked.

"I wanted to find out whose cupcakes were better," Aunt Patsy said with a smile, "mine or the great Famous François's!"

She nodded at the table of kids, even though they couldn't see her. "So I invited my best customers for a little taste test," she added.

"A taste test?" asked Nancy. "So you never cut a chunk out of Famous François's wedding cake?"

"Absolutely not!" Aunt Patsy said. "As a baker myself, I could never ruin a cake!"

Nancy believed her.

And she believed in Aunt Patsy's cupcakes.

"You don't need a taste test, Patsy," said Nancy. "All the kids in River Heights think your cupcakes rule."

"Really?" Aunt Patsy asked excitedly. She turned to the table. "Is that true, kids? Are my cupcakes the best?"

"Sure!" Marcy said. "But can we please have some already?"

"And can we take off our blindfolds?" Quincy asked. "Mine itches!"

"Of course!" said Aunt Patsy. "Forget the taste test. Instead, it's cupcakes all around!"

The kids cheered as they yanked off their blindfolds.

"Would you like some cupcakes too?" Aunt Patsy asked the girls.

"Yes!" Bess answered.

"No, thank you," Nancy said. "We ate a ton of sweet stuff last night."

"So did Bess," George added, pulling her cousin away from the table.

As they made their way through the store, Bess complained, "Why couldn't we have cup-cakes?"

"Because we have to work on this case," Nancy said. "Aunt Patsy is innocent, so the only suspect we have left is—"

*BUMP!* Nancy gasped as she crashed into

someone. Looking up, she saw Mr. Kernkraut!

He was wearing a red parka and beige corduroy pants. His eyes widened as he stared at the girls.

"Hi, Mr. Kernkraut," George said. "Can we ask you about something that happened in the cake room last night?"

"I—I must be in the wrong place!" Mr. Kernkraut stammered. "I thought this was the fish store!"

He turned and hurried up the block.

"Did you see the way he looked when George

asked him about the cake room?" Bess asked.

"Yeah," said Nancy. She watched as Mr. Kernkraut skidded around a corner. "Like a guy with something to *hide*!"

# ChaPTER EiGhT

## Nose Knows

Nancy, Bess, and George discussed the case as they walked down River Street. It was an extra-cold day, so their breath came out in wispy white clouds.

"We know Mr. Kernkraut was in the cake room, because we found his tie in the trash can," Nancy said.

"Aunt Patsy said the cake room was locked," George recalled. "And Mr. Kernkraut had the key."

The pom-pom on Bess's hat jiggled as she turned to Nancy. "We know he was snacking at the wedding," she said. "Would he take a bite out of the wedding cake, too?"

"Maybe," said Nancy. She rubbed her chin with her mitten as she thought. "I wonder if the cream on Mr. Kernkraut's tie is the same cream that was on the cake."

"Too bad we don't have a piece of the wedding cake to see," Bess said.

"We do have a piece!" said George. "My mom didn't want to waste the wedding cake, so she cut some slices and brought them home."

"Where are they?" Nancy asked.

"In our freezer," George told her. "I ate a slice last night. The cherry filling was awesome!"

Bess stopped walking.

"Wait a minute," she said with a frown. "I'll taste the cake—but no way am I tasting the cream on that tie!"

"Me neither," George chimed in. "That's even too gross for me!"

Nancy agreed. There had to be another way!

❀  ❀  ❀

"Eww!" Nancy cried after opening the plastic bag holding the tie. The cream had become crusty and funky-smelling.

Nancy pressed the bag shut. It was Saturday night, but she didn't want to watch TV or play a game with her dad. All she wanted to do was think about the case.

"Too bad you're not Henry the Hero Hound, Chip." Nancy sighed. She tossed the plastic bag on her desk. "Then you could sniff the tie and the cake and see if it's a match."

Chip padded over to Nancy's desk. With her paws against the desk, Chip jumped up and sniffed the plastic bag. Her tail was wagging as if she didn't mind the smell.

"Unless," Nancy said slowly, "you're more like Henry the Hero Hound than I thought!"

Nancy raced downstairs to the kitchen phone and called George. Without even saying hello, Nancy explained what she had in mind.

"Bring a slice of cake to River Street tomorrow morning," she told George. "I'll bring the icky tie."

"Don't tell me we're going to do a taste test!" George cried.

"Nope," said Nancy. "We're going to do a sniff test!"

"Chip better not have a cold!" Bess said. "Her nose has to work perfectly!"

"It will," Nancy said, clutching Chip's leash.

It was Sunday morning. Mrs. Fayne had a catering job on River Street, so she drove the three girls there too. Chip was allowed in the van as long as she didn't sit near the food.

"What should I do?" asked George. Between her gloved hands was a piece of wedding cake wrapped in clear plastic.

"Unwrap the cake," Nancy directed. "Then

stand at the end of the block with it."

George began unwrapping the cake as she walked to the end of the block.

Nancy pulled the tie out of the bag. She held it right in front of Chip's nose.

"Take a good whiff, Chip!" Nancy said. She then whipped the tie away. "Now track that scent, girl!"

Chip let out a bark and kicked up her hind legs. Then, like a rocket, she took off down River Street.

"She's running straight toward George!" Bess squealed.

"Good girl, Chip!" Nancy shouted. "Good girl!"

Chip bolted toward George and the cake. But halfway down the block, the puppy screeched to a stop. Her ears flopped as she made a sharp turn.

"Why did she stop?" asked Bess.

Nancy watched as her puppy charged through the open door of a store. It was the Hole in One Bagel Store.

The girls ran after Chip and into the store. The place was filled with people buying bagels and eating at small tables and chairs. But where was Chip?

"Woof, woof!"

Nancy turned to a nearby table. Chip was barking and jumping up at a man eating a bagel.

"She wants my bagel and cream cheese!" the man cried.

Nancy was too confused to do anything. Why was Chip going after cream cheese?

*Unless,* Nancy thought, looking at the tie in her hand, *that's what this icky stain is!*

# CHAPTER NINE

## Art Smart

"Somebody grab that dog!" the man behind the counter shouted. "And get it out of here!"

Nancy tossed the tie to Bess. Then she ran to Chip, grabbed her collar, and tugged.

"Down, Chip!" Nancy scolded. "Down!"

Chip finally stopped jumping. Clipping the leash onto the collar, Nancy quickly walked Chip out of the store. Bess and George followed.

"Will someone please take this thing?" Bess said, holding up the tie. "It's totally gross!"

Nancy was about to take it when a woman's voice said, "Bob, isn't that your tie?"

Nancy turned and saw Mr. Kernkraut. A

woman wearing a black coat and a pink fleece hat was standing next to him.

"Hello, Mr. Kernkraut!" Nancy called.

"Oh, hi," said Mr. Kernkraut, not really smiling. "This is my wife, Maureen."

"And that's your tie, Bob!" Mrs. Kernkraut exclaimed. She pointed to the tie in Bess's hand. "I gave it to you for that snowball wedding you worked on!"

Beads of sweat began dotting Mr. Kernkraut's

face. "It's like this, Maureen," he said. "I got a humongous stain on the tie, so I had to throw it away."

"We found it in a trash can," Nancy explained. "Is the stain on it cream cheese?"

"Um," Mr. Kernkraut started to say.

"Cream cheese?" Mrs. Kernkraut gasped. "That isn't on the Waist Watchers diet, Bob."

"It . . . isn't?" Mr. Kernkraut asked.

"Have you been snacking on the job?" demanded Mrs. Kernkraut. "Go on, Bob, spill."

"I-i-it was just a cracker with cream cheese and salmon!" Mr. Kernkraut stammered. "Very high in protein!"

"Wow!" said Bess. "Chip really did track the scent—just like Henry the Hero Hound!"

"And the stain on Mr. Kernkraut's tie was never wedding cake cream," George said. "It was cream cheese!"

"Wedding cake?" Mrs. Kernkraut said. "Bob, don't tell me you were eating cake, too?"

"Never!" Mr. Kernkraut insisted.

Nancy didn't want to get Mr. Kernkraut into trouble, but if she was going to solve the case, she had to ask more questions.

"But if you weren't eating cake, what were you doing in the cake room?" she asked. "That's where we found your tie in the trash can."

Mr. Kernkraut took a deep breath. Then he said, "I didn't want anyone to see me eating the cream cheese cracker, so I hid inside the cake room. When I got the stain on my tie, I threw it away."

"Oh, Bob." Mrs. Kernkraut sighed. "Next you're going to tell me you've been eating cupcakes!"

Mr. Kernkraut stared bug-eyed at the girls. The girls stared back. That's when it clicked.

"So that's why you looked so scared when you saw us at the bakery yesterday," Bess said with a smile. "You were there to buy cupcakes!"

Chip growled at Mr. Kernkraut.

"Come on, Bob," said Mrs. Kernkraut gently. "We can still make the Sunday morning Waist Watchers meeting!"

"Fine with me," Mr. Kernkraut agreed. "I'm tired of being sneaky. From now on I want to be healthy!"

But as the couple began walking away Nancy called, "Wait, please!"

"Now what?" Mr. Kernkraut asked.

"Did anyone else have a key to the cake room beside you?" Nancy asked.

"Just the baker, François," said Mr. Kernkraut. "I gave him the extra key in case he had to get to his cake."

The Kernkrauts hooked arms as they walked away.

"Bess, George," Nancy said. "Do you think Famous François ruined his own wedding cake?"

"Anything is possible," said George. "That François is as flaky as his pie crusts!"

The girls walked Chip back to the Drew house. Once upstairs, George looked up the address of François's studio. She found it on the baker's own website.

"His studio is practically in the next town," George said. "That's way out of our walking rules."

Nancy looked over George's shoulder at François's home page. It had French music playing over it. And pictures of cakes to click on for prices, special events, and directions. Nancy grabbed the mouse and clicked on the cake marked Special Events.

A new page opened. Nancy read the announcement on the screen. "Famous François is having a special show for his cakes today," she said. "And it's in the River Heights Art Gallery on Bank Street!"

"Bank Street is only four blocks away," said George.

"We can do it!" Nancy said happily.

"But why is he showing his cakes at an art gallery instead of a bakery?" Bess asked.

With a French accent, George exclaimed, "Because he eez not just a baker—he eez zee Famous François!"

The girls got permission to ride their bikes to Bank Street. They parked outside the art gallery and watched the people as they went inside. Everyone looked artsy in their black clothes.

But as the girls approached the entrance, Nancy saw something that made her heart sink. It was a sign in front of the door that read NO CHILDREN UNDER AGE 12 ALLOWED.

"No kids?" Nancy complained.

"Who do they think eats cake, anyway?" George said.

A man wearing a black wool coat and a silky scarf stood directly in front of the door. The name tag stuck on his coat read STEPHEN ARMSTRONG.

"He looks like he's guarding the door," George said.

"Maybe he's nice and will let us in," said Nancy.

A family walked up to the door. Stephen looked at their two little kids and shook his head. The family walked away.

"Or maybe not." Nancy sighed.

"Watch this, you guys," George said with a grin.

Nancy and Bess followed George to the door. George looked up at Stephen and said, "Hi, Mr. Armstrong. Did you see my baby brother?"

Stephen peered down his nose at George. "Baby brother?" he asked with a sniff.

"Yeah," George said. "He just ran past you into the gallery."

"And he loves cake!" Bess added with a smile.

Stephen's eyes popped wide open. Through gritted teeth he hissed, "Go in there and get him out. Now!"

"Yes, sir!" said George.

The girls slipped past the guard into the gallery. They were in!

"Good thinking, George!" Nancy whispered.

The girls looked around. Guests were sipping fruit punch and coffee out of small plastic cups. They walked slowly around cakes shaped like everything from the Statue of Liberty to the presidents on Mount Rushmore.

"Fabulous!" one man was saying.

"He's not a baker," a woman swooned. "He's a modern-day Michelangelo!"

Famous François stood in the back of the studio, talking to a woman holding a writing pad. Nancy guessed she was a reporter.

"Look! There's Adele," Bess whispered.

Nancy looked to see where Bess was pointing. Through the crowd she could see Adele serving a plate of cookies to the guests.

A woman wearing a black dress and a pearl necklace waved her hands in the air and said, "And now, a word from the artist himself—Famous François!"

The guests crowded around François as he started to speak. "I was just a wee boy in Paris when I baked my first cookie. My mama tasted it—and began to cry!"

"Everyone's listening to François," Nancy whispered. "Now's a good time to look for clues!"

Nancy, Bess, and George walked slowly around the towering cakes. They stopped at one shaped like a big castle. On the top were colorful flags and banners.

"François likes to put stuff on the tops of his cakes," Nancy pointed out. "Just like those ice wolves."

"The cakes are so high!" said Bess. "How does he get up there?"

"There was no ladder in the cake room," Nancy pointed out.

"He could have stepped on the cart," George said.

The girls exchanged looks as they all remembered the creamy footprint.

"Maybe that footprint was François's!" said Nancy.

"Yeah," George said. "He could have stepped up on the cart like this . . ."

Nancy and Bess gasped as George jumped up on the cart.

"George! That's dangerous!"

"It's okay, the wheels are locked. Then François could have reached way up," George said. She stretched her arm above her head. "Just like this—whoooooaaaa!"

As George lost her balance, her foot sank into the side of the cake!

"Oh, no!" Nancy groaned.

But as George jumped off the cart, she left a creamy footprint on the tablecloth. It was at the

bottom of the cake—just like the one they found near the wedding cake.

"You see?" George said, pointing to the footprint. "That's how Famous François ruined his own wedding cake!"

Then—

"My Crème de la Castle!" a voice cried. "What did they do to my Crème de la Castle?"

The three friends whirled around.

Famous François was standing behind them with his hands on his hips. And he looked mad!

# CHAPTER TEN

## Case Cracked

"How did these girls get in here?" François demanded.

"I—I—I," Stephen stammered.

Adele squeezed her way through the crowd, still holding the plate of cookies. Nancy noticed that she was not wearing fancy clothes. Instead Adele wore black pants, a striped blouse, and the same white canvas sneakers she'd worn at the wedding. Then Nancy noticed something about the sneakers. One had a dark pink stain across the toe. Dark pink—like cherry filling!

"What's going on?" Adele asked.

"We're detectives," said Bess.

"You mean you're playing detective!" the

woman with the pearl necklace said.

"This isn't a game, ma'am," George told her. "We're the Clue Crew."

"And we're trying to find out what happened to François's wedding cake on Friday night," Nancy explained.

"I thought you looked familiar!" François said with narrowed eyes. "You're the children from the wedding. The ones who ruined my cake!"

"We didn't do it," Nancy said calmly. "We think someone stepped on the table to decorate the top."

"Then accidentally stepped into the cake," Bess added.

"Ridiculous!" François said. "My cake was completely decorated by me. From the cupcakes at the base to the ice wolves of Patagonia at the top!"

"Ice wolves instead of a bride and groom!" a man declared. "Brilliant!"

*A bride and groom*, Nancy suddenly thought. *Just like the bride and groom in Adele's pocket!*

"Adele!" Nancy blurted.

Adele was so startled by Nancy's voice that she dropped her plate of cookies.

"Sorry, Adele," said Nancy. "But did you try to take the ice wolves off of Sara's wedding cake?"

"And did you step on the wedding cake by accident?" Bess asked.

"Like I just did?" George said, pointing to the castle cake.

"You girls are leaving right now!" Stephen ordered. He was about to grab their shoulders when Adele stepped forward.

"Wait!" she shouted.

Stephen froze. All eyes were on Adele as her shoulders dropped.

"It *was* an accident," Adele said. "I was only trying to help Sara."

"What?" François gasped.

"It was Sara's wedding and it should have been perfect," Adele explained. "So I went into the cake room and tried to replace the wolves with a bride and groom."

Nancy stared at Adele. She was confessing!

"As I was climbing to reach the wolves, my foot slipped inside the cake," Adele said. "It was a big hole, so I cut around it to make it look like someone cut a piece."

"What about the wolves?" asked Bess.

"I stuck the bride and groom in my pocket," Adele admitted. "And left those tacky wolves on the cake."

"Tacky wolves?" François cried. "They were my vision!"

"But it wasn't about you, Dad," Adele said gently. "It was about Sara and Brett."

Adele then turned to the guests.

"Everything else about the snowball wedding was perfect," she said. She smiled at George. "George's mother did a super job catering the affair."

George turned to the reporter with a smile. "That's Mrs. Fayne of Fayne's Catering Service!" she said. "It's spelled F-A-Y-N-E!"

As the reporter scribbled on her pad, Adele shook her head sadly.

"I'm sorry I let my dad blame everyone else," she said. "And I'm sorry I ruined the cake— even if it was an accident."

Then Adele folded her arms and continued. "But when I become a famous baker like my dad, I'm going to make sure the customer is always right!"

The guests smiled as they applauded Adele.

"Oh, I suppose my daughter is right," François admitted. "From now on, Famous François will put the customer first too!"

Nancy smiled. Famous François may have taught Adele how to bake. But Adele taught her dad how to be nice!

"By the way," François said, "since my daughter was brave enough to confess, I want to confess too."

Nancy, Bess, and George traded puzzled looks. Confess to what? And what happened to his French accent?

"I'm not really François from Paris, France," François said. "I'm Frank from Bayonne, New Jersey. But hey, I'm still a genius, right?"

The woman with the pearls stepped up to the Crème de la Castle cake. "Should I take this cake away, François—I mean Frank?" she asked. "It's totally ruined."

"Nah," said Frank. "Cut up the top part and serve it to the guests. Cakes should be eaten!"

The guests let out a cheer. But Stephen marched straight over to Nancy, Bess, and George. "I'll show these girls out right away," he said.

"Forget about it!" Frank boomed. "Not only can they stay, I'll bake each of their birthday cakes this year!"

"Yippeeee!" Nancy cheered.

The three friends grabbed hands and jumped up and down. They had solved a mystery—and

they were going to get the birthday cakes of their dreams!

They stopped jumping as Adele walked over.

"It's so cool that you guys are detectives," she said. "Solving mysteries must be so hard!"

"Not this mystery," Nancy said with a smile. "This one was a *piece of cake!*"

# Basket Case!

Guess what? You don't have to be a flower girl like Nancy to carry a petal-pretty basket—or to keep a handy basket on your dresser to hold your favorite things. And the best news is, you can make it yourself!

### You Will Need:

1 basket in any color (or ask an adult to help you spray-paint a plain one)
¾" to 2" white lace ribbons
String of small pearl-style beads
Narrow ribbon in your favorite color
Plastic or silk flowers
Craft glue

# Ready? Now get a handle on your basket!

❀ Glue one or two of your lace ribbons around the basket.

❀ Wrap the narrow ribbon tightly around the basket handle. Leave the ends long enough to hang as trailers.

❀ Wrap the string of beads around the handle over the ribbon. Be careful not to wrap too tightly, or the beads might pop off. Oops!

❀ Use the glue to attach the silk or plastic flowers to the ends of the handles or around the bottom of the basket.

❀ You don't have to stop there. Add sequins, silver or gold paper stars, glitter, curly ribbons— or decorate your basket with tons of stickers!

# Fill 'Er Up!

❀ Your basket may be finished, but the fun has just begun. Fill your crafty creation with flower petals, cookies, photographs, hair accessories, jewelry, your favorite stuffed animals, even your own creamy cupcakes to deliver to your BFFs—anything but onions!

# NANCY DREW
## AND THE CLUE CREW®

## Can you solve these other mysteries from Nancy Drew and the Clue Crew?

#13 *Chick-napped!*
1-4169-5522-4 (paperback)

#14 *The Zoo Crew*
1-4169-5899-1 (paperback)

#15 *Mall Madness*
1-4169-5900-9 (paperback)

#16 *Thanksgiving Thief*
1-4169-6777-X (paperback)

## Collect them all!

A new graphic novel every 3 months!
Collect them all!

At your favorite bookstore or order from Papercutz, 40 Exchange Place, Ste. 1308, New York, NY 10005, 1-800-886-1223 MC, VISA, AMEX accepted, add $4 P&H for first book, $1 each additional. Make checks payable to NBM. Distributed by Macmillan.

PAPERCUTZ.com